Everything Bad Happens To Jeremiah Riddle

Brad D. Sibbersen

THE SUN had just reached its apex when the old roan wavered and went down on both front knees. Jeremiah dismounted just in time to avoid a broken leg – or worse – because moments later the horse toppled over on its left side and was still. "Ya done good, girl," Jeremiah said, patting the animal on her side. She was still breathing shallowly, so he put her out of her misery, then dug out his canteen and lifted it to his parched lips. Halfway through the motion he realized that it felt a mite insubstantial, and when he examined it he found the clean, round bullet hole, not quite four hours old. "Ya missed, Jonah, ya ugly cuss," he said out loud. "But ya mighta killed me anyway." Tossing the useless canteen aside he gathered what he could easily carry – six shooters, bed roll – and continued across the desert on foot.

Heat, dehydration, and exhaustion collected their debts in short order. Within the hour he had a headache to beat all, and after four he started seeing things. A shimmer, always just at the edge of his vision, suggesting cavorting falls of crisp, clean water, surrounded by lush green foliage dripping with moisture. Shadowy figures that disappeared when he looked directly at them. At one point a phantom tumbleweed rolled lazily past him in the opposite direction, against the wind. The vultures that were circling him now were probably real enough. Not that it mattered either way.

As the sun dipped towards the horizon the wind started picking up, and soon it was whipping up blinding whorls of sand that impeded his halting progress even more. He wrapped a kerchief around his nose and mouth, pulled his hat low, and pressed the fancy tinted eyeglasses he wore flush against his face, but the sand still found its way into his eyes, his nose, his throat. After a time he resigned himself to the fact that each step was his last, but he always managed just one more, and uncountable hours later, after the sun had fallen and risen again, freezing him to the bone in the interim, his tenacity paid off when something that resembled civilization coalesced out of the maelstrom. A score of buildings, facing each other across an expanse of packed earth suggesting a road, where a liberated rain barrel danced back and forth, battered by the shifting winds. A wooden sign that read "OUTSKIRTS" banged repeatedly against the weather-beaten building where it hung from two rusty eye bolts. There was a hotel/saloon, but it was shut up tight, the watering trough out front half-filled with sand. All the buildings, it seemed, were shut up tight. Where were all the people? A sheet of newsprint fluttered by on the wind, caught on a hitching post, and Jeremiah snatched it up before the wind could claim it again. *The Weekly Outskirter*, the masthead proclaimed. *Outskirts, Arizona – July 7, 1881.* Today's date. So now he knew where he was. Far more compelling, however, was the story dominating the front page:

Every Man, Woman, and Child on Earth Disappears!

"What th' holy hell?" Jeremiah whispered to himself.

"Hey, mister, ain't you got no sense to come in outta the wind?" someone shouted.

The slim young man the voice belonged to ushered Jeremiah through the door and slammed it shut behind them, barring it securely against the storm. A large, functional desk dominated the room he found himself in, flanked on one side by a Daughaday printing press and on the other by stacks and stacks of printed news sheets that matched the one in his hand. The papers were freshly printed, the press itself quite new. The young man's hands were stained with ink, and his spectacles were askew, but he couldn't have looked happier. "Welcome to the offices of the Outskirts *Outskirter*!" he beamed. He indicated the sheet in Jeremiah's hand.

"Looks like you're my first-ever customer!"

"I ain't got two cents," Jeremiah said.

"Keep it. Gratis."

Jeremiah studied the paper in his hand again.

"Looks like my presence is puttin' th' lie t' yer big story," he said. "Never mind yer own."

"Oh, well..." the young man blushed. "See, it's not really a newspaper. I mean, I'm not printing real news, as it were." He grew excited again. "I'm a purveyor of *speculative fiction*."

"So, lies."

"Excuse me?"

"*Fiction* is lies."

"Well, I suppose, but this is *speculative* fiction."

"Fancy lies."

The young man deflated slightly, and Jeremiah figured he'd twisted him long enough.

"So what is spec'utive fiction?" he asked.

"They're stories," the young man explained, "about things that might happen in the *future*. Or stories about amazing new inventions, and their inventors. Adventure stories, essentially, but with a firm foundation in *science*."

"I see. Spec'utive fiction."

"S-F for short."

Jeremiah mulled this over.

"*Ess-Eff* ain't memorable an' it's hard to say. Ya oughta call it..." he brainstormed for a moment "...*Spec-Fic*."

The young man frowned at this appellation. He quickly changed the subject by extending his hand and belatedly introducing himself.

"Harold Artemis Faust, author/publisher extraordinaire, at your service. Art, if you prefer."

"Jeremiah Riddle, all-around malcontent." They shook.

"So why don't ya put yer stories in books?" Jeremiah asked.

"Binding books is expensive. Not that this press was cheap – it cost me eighteen dollars! – but now, for the cost of the paper and ink, I can print up a run of one of my stories any time I like. And I got to thinking, why not lay it out like it was a real newspaper, full of news stories that aren't real stories but are..."

"Spec'utive fiction."

"Right!"

"Well," Jeremiah said, "yer not off t' a very good start."

"How do you figure?"

"If every man, woman, and child done disappeared, then who printed this story about it?"

Art's face blanched noticeably.

"You'll have to read it to find out," he quickly said, not a little defensively.

"Okeh," Jeremiah said, folding the sheet under his arm. "Ya done me a solid so I'll do that. And I'll pass it on t' th' next fella I meet who might want t' enjoy some *spec'utive fiction.*"

"Thank you!" Art grinned. "How'd you find yourself on foot in that habūb, anyhow?"

"Haboob?"

"Dust storm. That's what the Arabs call it."

"Had a horse keel over unnerneath me."

"Shame. Well you're lucky you stumbled across us. If you'd missed Outskirts there's nothing but desert until Yuma, and you'd be dead by then."

Jeremiah nodded. He couldn't disagree with that logic.

As it turned out though, "lucky" was relative.

II

THE TWO OF THEM retreated to Art's room upstairs, where he produced a bottle of palatable whiskey and poured them both a heaping glass. "Hope it's not too early for you," he told Jeremiah. "It would be for me, but I've been up all night." They discussed the town, what there was to discuss, because it was less a town than a way station, a convenient stopping point for people on their way to California – San Diego, specifically. "I predict San Diego is going to be the capital of California some day," Art said, tipping his glass to Jeremiah. "You mark my words." His plan was to distribute his "speculative fiction" newspapers to anyone and everyone passing through to San Diego, on the assumption that sheer boredom would move them to read the things during the final leg of their journey. Then, with any luck, they'd talk the stories up once they reached their destination, spreading his fame throughout the city. "Once I create enough demand, I'm hoping to relocate there," Art concluded.

"As good a plan as any," Jeremiah acquiesced.

By eight o'clock, the dust storm had abated.

"I'm gonna need t' earn a handful," Jeremiah said as they stepped outside. The town was slowly coming back to life. "Enough t' buy a horse, or passage on th' next stage that comes through."

"Well, there's always something needs doing. Let's take a walk around town."

At that moment, a man barreling by on the far side of the street glanced their way, did a double-take, and altered his trajectory to intercept them. Easily topping three hundred pounds, his clothes appeared freshly pressed, and his red, neatly-trimmed beard did nothing to belie his boyish features. The shiny gold star on his chest came as such a surprise that Jeremiah blinked and shook his head, just to make sure he wasn't still seeing things.

"Who's your friend?" the corpulent lawman asked Art.

"This is Mr. Jeremiah Riddle. He lost his horse in the desert."

"I'm gonna have to ask you where you were last night," the sheriff said to Jeremiah.

"Out there," Jeremiah said, hooking a thumb over his shoulder in the direction of said desert.

"I'll vouch for him," Art said. The sheriff gave the itinerant the once-over and decided that he was bedraggled and dusty enough for his story to be true.

"Okeh." He dismissed Jeremiah and addressed

Art. "I had to ask because it happened again! One of George Bartlett's this time. I'm heading over there to check it out right now. I know you like this queer stuff, so you can come along if you like."

"Queer stuff?" Jeremiah asked. He followed Art, who followed the sheriff.

"Real queer," Art enthused. "Someone..." he paused for effect "...or some *thing* has been tearing up horses – three so far. And one person, we think. The town drunk. Got him when he passed out behind the saloon one night."

"We got no shortage of town drunks," the sheriff interjected. A strange juxtaposition, his soft appearance and this cold-blooded, no-nonsense dismissal.

George Bartlett's stables were a fifteen minute walk from town proper, and when the trio arrived George was waiting for them, fit to be tied. "'Bout time you waddled out here, Sheriff!" he shouted. The dead horse was in the yard, several hundred feet from the stable. Stripped to the bone in several places, one of its rear legs missing entirely, its death was obviously the work of a predator.

"I lost 'er in the storm last night, found 'er like this!" George grumbled. "It's those Apache. They're fuckin' cannibals, you know, the lot of 'em."

"*Cannibalism* implies an inter-species act..." Art began.

"Sheriff, what is he doin' here?" George

groaned. "I ain't in the mood for all his *facts*."

"I'm an interested party," Art said, folding his arms.

"All right, all right," said the sheriff, holding his hands up in a warding-off gesture. "No need for everybody to get all riled up. Art, run back to town, get my horse, and round up two, three layabouts. Tell 'em I'll pay 'em one dollar for a day's work. We'll scour the area, see what we can find."

"I could use a dollar, Sheriff," Jeremiah said.

"You're hired." The sheriff extended his hand. "Cason Merrick. Case, if you like."

"Jeremiah Riddle."

They shook.

"I'll be your third," Art volunteered. "If we borrow three of George's horses, it'll save us some time."

"This lumberin' tub mounts one of my horses, I'll have two dead," George said, indicating the sheriff.

"All right, that's enough!" Case snapped. George grinned, pleased to have gotten the sheriff's goat. "We'll borrow two of yours, I'll ride my own! Art, run fetch Giant."

"You borry two of my horses, I'm coming with you," George insisted.

"Fine! As long as you keep that fly-catcher of yours shut!"

This was going to be one hard-earned dollar, Jeremiah reflected.

III

THE FOURSOME rode northwest, following the sheriff's lead. Soon, a plateau of red, striated rock rose out of the desert, looming over the dunes of sand formed against it by the storm. "We'll check the canyon first," Case said. "It's the only place anywhere near town where a big predator might be holed up."

George frowned. He was still fully committed to his Apache theory.

The drifted mounds of loose sand gave the horses pause, so Case left their mounts in George's charge and led the other two men up and over the dunes – their legs sometimes sinking to the knee – into a narrow canyon that split the plateau down the middle.

"Doesn't look like anything lives here," Jeremiah said.

"You'd be surprised," said Art. "Life finds a way. Adapts. You familiar with the theory of evolution?"

"Can't say as I am."

"It suggests that everything, every living thing,

13

comes from something else, because each generation is born just a little different."

"So a big ol' crocodile might have a little ol' gecko as a great-great-grandparent? Or versa-vica?"

"Something like that," Art nodded.

"Okeh," Case said, "start looking for hollows, overhangs, any hidey-hole where something might've set up shop. I'm guessing we're looking for a puma, or maybe a bobcat with delusions of grandeur." He'd brought a rifle, a Winchester repeater, so he passed his six-shooter to Art, who accepted it reluctantly. "If it's here, it's cornered, so we shoot first and sort out the details later, got it?"

The other two men nodded.

Slowly they made their way along the narrow passage, eyeing every nook and cranny, pulling their hats low to shield their eyes when the sun rose high enough to find its way into the canyon.

Jeremiah froze, shocked, when the other two men walked right past it.

There was a *door* in the cliff face.

And not some jury-rigged trap door, either – a proper *door*, with a turn handle and everything, set into the rock. Case and Art had strolled right by without comment, as if it wasn't even there.

Jeremiah closed his eyes, shook his head, opened them again.

The door was gone.

Lack of sleep and the oppressive heat were taking their toll – he was seeing things. Or maybe it was the quarter bottle of whiskey he'd downed for breakfast. Either way, he reflected that he was likely losing his mind as he stepped up to the rock and placed his palm, flat, against it. Just to be sure. There was nothing here. Just rough, red stone.

And yet...

"Son of a bitch...!" The sheriff's voice, distraught, from up ahead. Jeremiah hurried to catch up.

The canyon culminated in a dead end. Particularly so for the man they found there.

Skeletonized, his bones already bleached where the noonday sun could reach them. His clothes and hat were tatters. A dented canteen lay nearby, and in one bony hand, his right, a six-shooter. Jeremiah's eyes darted around and he immediately located three bullets the man had apparently fired at... something. His keen eye even pinpointed the place where one of these bullets had ricocheted off the canyon wall. The dead man's final shot had punched a gaping hole in his own skull. He'd apparently fired this one upwards, through the roof of his mouth.

"Ya know this man?" Jeremiah asked.

"Hard to say," Case frowned, kneeling beside the remains. "The local scavengers have stripped him pretty clean." He stood, considered Jeremiah. "You say you was alone when you... lost your horse?'

The two men locked eyes, each waiting for the other to do something stupid. When neither did, they both relaxed.

"S'truth, Sheriff. I don't know this man."

"No one's missing from town," Art interjected.

"That we know of." The sheriff's frown deepened. "Someone left this man here to die, or they did him in proper and then made it look like he done it himself. Either way it's murder."

"Looks like he was shooting at somethin' at th' end," Jeremiah said, pointing out the discharged bullets. "What do ya suppose that might've been?"

"Maybe the ones that done him in. Or maybe a vulture that arrived too early for dinner. Bullets might not even be his."

"It don't smack right, Sheriff," Jeremiah said. "Bushwhackin' a man and leavin' him in a state where he ain't one hunnerd percent dead. And still packin' a loaded iron yet."

"You speaking from experience, Mr. Riddle?"

"I'm speakin' from common sense."

"Whatever the case, this is gonna have to take precedence." Case looked up at the sky. "It's near noon. Way I see it, you boys have earned fifty cents of that dollar. You help me get what's left of this fella back to town, I'll pay you in full."

"Ya drive a hard bargain, Sheriff," Jeremiah grumbled.

||||

REVERENCE GAVE WAY to practicality when Art returned with the news that no one in town was unaccounted for. Rolling the skeleton up in the old blanket he'd been sent to fetch, they secured it with rope and draped it over one of the horses.

"I'm gonna have Doc Hathaway give them bones a look-over," Case said to no one in particular as they made their way back. "Maybe there's somethin' to 'em that we missed."

"Perceptive fella, this Hathaway?" Jeremiah asked. There was a tingling at the back of his neck, and he wanted to keep the conversation going, in large part, to drown it out. Truth be told, he felt like they were being watched. No, not watched. Stalked. His eyes scanned the flat, scrubby landscape all around them, again and again. Dry, baked earth. Tufts of jaundiced desert grass. In the distance a tumbleweed briefly paced them before coming up against a gnarled desert ironwood. There was simply nothing there. There couldn't be, because there was nowhere for a body to hide. And yet...

"He's a good man," Case said.

"Yuma stage is late," Art offered, changing the subject.

Case grunted noncommittally.

"Damned Yuma stage is always late," George griped.

"There's folks camped in front of Mae's, waiting."

"Let 'em wait."

George pulled up as they came parallel to his place. They were returning to town as the crow flies, same as Art had done when he'd fetched the blanket, and the stables were south of them now.

"I'd like to stable my horses, Sheriff. Your men can walk from here."

Case considered for a moment.

"You willin' to hire 'em out for the day?" the sheriff asked. He indicated their gruesome cargo. "I'd like to look into this further, and I could use the assist."

"To Mark Twain here, sure," George said, referring to Art. "But I don't know this other fella from Judas. What if he runs off with my property?"

"I'll see to it that he don't."

"You do that," George said, shooting Jeremiah a look. *"Hyah!"* he urged his horse, and was off in a cloud of dust.

"He gives me such a pain..." Case shook his head.

There was a modicum of bustle as they rode back into town. There weren't a lot of people out and about – because there were, quite simply, not a lot of people – but those that did live and work in Outskirts all seemed to be going somewhere or doing something. It took Jeremiah a minute or so of disinterested observing to realize that most of them were milling about aimlessly, casually socializing, or just wandering around. Four easterners – you could tell by their clothes – loitered in front of the hotel/saloon, sitting on trunks and clutching carpet bags, their demeanor irritable and accusatory.

"Late stage always throws people off," Art explained.

"Hey, sheriff!" one of the easterners called out as the trio passed. Case aggressively ignored him. At the far end of the street he pulled up and dismounted in front of the pharmacy, and the other two men followed suit.

"Take our friend inside," Case said. "I'll secure the horses."

"Sheriff!" the easterner called out again. Now he was coming this way. Case sighed, pretended not to hear.

"Locked up tight!" Art said, indicating the pharmacy.

Case waved them to the next door to the left, and the party barged through unceremoniously.

"Tarnation, this is a home! Around back! Around back!"

"Time is of the essence, Heddy," the sheriff said, warding off the heavyset woman confronting them with a wave of his hand. She shook a wooden spoon at the lot of them as Jeremiah and Art carried their burden through the cramped drawing room. Two young children, a boy and a girl, gaped. A door at the far end up the room opened into a short hallway that led to Hathaway's tiny examination room at the rear of the pharmacy. The doctor joined them moments later, his white-grey hair sticking up in a hundred directions, shaving soap still on his face.

"What's this, then?" he asked.

"You just get out of bed, Doc?" Case asked, mildly incredulous.

"Stage is late," the doctor huffed, as if this were a perfectly reasonable explanation.

"Found this fella out the canyon," Case explained as Jeremiah and Art placed the bundled skeleton on the examination table and carefully unwrapped it. "Wondered if you might have any insights?" Hathaway gave it a cursory glance.

"He's dead," the doctor said, frowning. "You know, there's a door 'round back, opens directly into this office. See it? Right there." He pointed it out.

"Now, Abner, you tell Heddy I'm sorry. It's just that..."

Apparently it was Heddy's turn to do the barging, because she did just that, bursting into the room and interrupting Case mid-sentence.

"Man out front, says he needs to speak to you, Sheriff!" she exclaimed.

"Tell him I'm busy and I'll be along."

"He's not coming inside! Got enough strangers marching through my house today!" She gave Jeremiah a dirty look.

"Okeh, Heddy," the doctor said dismissively.

"Don't you adopt that tone with me, Abner Hathaway!" She shook her spoon again.

"Heddy, please, this is important," pleaded Case. "A man's died."

"He'll be the first of many, this keeps up!" the woman declared as she retreated back into the house. Abner sighed.

"You see the trouble you bring down on me?" he said to Case.

"Save your marital jeremiad for your mistress," the sheriff said. "Can you tell me anything about this fella? Aside from what done him in, because we pretty well know that."

"Mistress," Abner snorted. "At *my* age." He bent over the bones on the table. "I know this man?" he asked perfunctorily.

"Doubtful," Case said.

"I guess you know he shot himself, or someone did it for him. Bones have been gnawed on. See these marks?" Case nodded. "Teeth. Desert scavengers, I'd reckon. Where'd you find him?"

"Out the canyon."

"What do you think was chewing on him, Doc?" Art asked.

"Whatever was hungry. Not much else I..."

They were interrupted by an excited banging from the front of the building. Someone pounding on the front door.

"Look," Abner said, "I got to open up the pharmacy before the stage arrives. Sounds as if they're like to knock the door in already. This man'll keep, obviously, if you want me to look him over some more, but I can give you my diagnosis now, and it's not likely to change."

Case nodded for him to go on.

"Fellow was either depressed or had enemies. After he done himself or was done in, desert critters ate him. Now you all need to be on your way. I got a business to run."

"You want we should take them bones with us?" Case asked as Abner steered them away from the hallway that led to his drawing room and ushered them into the pharmacy proper. He unlocked the front door to a frowning man who was making a show of looking at his pocket watch.

"They're not going anywhere. Come back around closing, I'll help you with 'em myself."

"Sheriff!" someone shouted the moment they were outside. The easterner was striding towards them, a look of determination on his face.

It was going to be a long day, Case reflected.

卌

"JOHNNY LOVE," the easterner said by way of introduction. His hat and clothes were cowboy-fashionable, big-city nonsense, fussy and immaculate. The pearl-handled Smith & Wesson he wore glinted in the sun and looked like it had spent most of its life in a velvet-lined box. An accessory. His broad smile and proffered hand did little to mask his current state of irritation.

"Something I can help you with?" Case asked. He refrained from shaking the man's hand.

"Well, Sheriff, I hope so. I need to be in San Diego by Friday morning and your stage from Yuma seems to be running mighty late."

"First of all, mister, it ain't *my* stage. And second, stages do run late. My suggestion is that you plan accordingly next time."

The man stared at him, taken aback by his bluntness. His smile wavered.

"If I could get that dollar, Sheriff, I'll be on my way," Jeremiah prodded.

"As you can see, I got business to attend to," Case told the man, seizing the out Jeremiah had

23

provided. "The stage will be along in due time."

"Well I was hoping there was someplace where I could buy a horse," Love persisted. "I got money. *Plenty* of money."

Jeremiah could almost hear unseen ears perk up at this.

"Well God bless you and yours," Case said. It was his polite way of saying "fuck you."

Doc Hathaway's two children picked this moment to explode out of their front door and surround the men, jumping up and down with the indefatigable energy of youth.

"Olly olly, olly olly!" they chanted.

"George might be willing to sell him a horse," Art offered. "If the price were right."

"Where can I find this George fellow?" Love asked Art, shooting Case a dirty look.

"Few minutes' walk outside of town. Ask anybody."

"Thanks." Doc's son pointed his index finger at the departing Love, thumb raised.

"Bang!" he said. Love smiled and returned the gesture.

"Bang!"

"He got me!" the boy cried, twirling and flailing around theatrically. "I'm kilt!" He fell to the ground. "I'm ded."

"I'm tellin'!" scolded his sister.

"Cason Merrick!" Heddy's voice drowned them all out as she appeared in the doorway. "Did you unload that mess of bones in Abner's office? *Human* bones? We'll have spooks for

certain, sure as I'm standin' here!"

"Bosh. There ain't no such," Case groaned.

"Now, we don't know that..." Art interjected.

"Mama! Henry's kilt! An' he's wearin' his Sunday clothes!"

"Boy!" Heddy shrieked. *"You get out them expensive clothes!!"*

"Right now?" Henry asked. He made as if to strip down right there in the street.

"Inside!!!"

"You're kilt and now you're in big trouble!" Henry's sister chided.

"People have photographed ghosts. Why, an Englishman named Sir William Crookes, a highly-respected chemist, was actually present when..."

There was a piercing scream then, from the other end of the street. Not a scream of anger or frustration, but a scream of honest terror.

It was a God-blessed relief.

$$\text{卌 I}$$

A MAN WAS STUMBLING out of the desert, into town. The scream had come from one of the easterners, who, playing to the gallery, subsequently swooned, only to hit the ground like a sack full of potatoes when her inattentive husband failed to catch her. Locals merely gawked as the ragged, tattered form took a few more halting steps, pirouetted, and collapsed to the ground. Art was the first to get to him. "Don't touch him!" Case shouted, huffing along behind. "Get the doctor!" he added, over his shoulder. Abner Hathaway appeared a moment later, summoned by Heddy, and joined them. Jeremiah, Abner's children, and several others crowded around.

"Too many..." the downed man croaked. He was covered with gashes and wounds, and his eyes had a filmy, far-way look.

"It's Frank Bilge," someone in the crowd exclaimed, "what drives the Yuma stage!"

Abner set his medical bag on the ground and opened it up. Kneeling down beside Bilge, he took out his stethoscope and checked the injured man's heartbeat.

"Erratic. Lot of blood loss. This man's dyin', no mind of what I do," the doctor declared.

"Too many what?" the sheriff asked, kneeling down on the other side of Bilge. "Too many *what?*"

"Too many injuns," someone in the crowd suggested. There was a titter of consent.

"Is that you?" Bilge said, looking past the sheriff at something only he could see. "It's you, innit?"

"It's Sheriff Merrick," Case said. But Frank wasn't talking to him.

"So beautiful and kind..." Frank went on, the hint of a smile on his thin, parched lips. "Can't believe I been afeared of you muh whole life..."

He expired.

"Who was he talkin' to?" Case asked the doctor.

"Delirium. It was just crazy talk."

"Those in'jries, they're not crazy talk," Jeremiah interjected.

"Let's just see here," Abner said, cutting the dead man's tattered shirt away with a scalpel. The more proper women averted their eyes.

"These are bite marks," the doctor said. "Something's been chewing on this man!"

"Scavengers?" Art ventured.

"While he was still alive and locomotin'?" scoffed Case. "Hardly seems likely."

"Maybe he fell, they got to him, and he got his

second wind."

"The real question," frowned the doctor, "is: Where's the stage?"

Case climbed to his feet.

"Art," he said, "I'm deputizin' you as of now." He turned to Jeremiah. "And you too, Mister, if you'll have it."

"Job pay?" Jeremiah asked.

"It does."

Jeremiah nodded his assent.

"Okeh. Mount up, boys. We need to locate that stage."

They overtook the impatient easterner, Johnny Love, en route, lugging his trunk in the direction of George's stable. He shook a fist at them as their passage coated his fancy dude attire with a kicked-up layer of trail dust.

Two hours of hard riding later, they found the stage.

One of the horses had apparently broken free and fled, it was nowhere to be seen. The others were dead, sliced to ribbons, their legs, specifically, stripped entirely to the bone. The only reason their collapsing weight hadn't flipped the stage itself on its side is because it had settled up in a shallow gully where it now rested, canted, one rear wheel entirely off the ground. The wheel opposite diagonal, meanwhile, was cracked near in half. A bloody, gory mess that had once been the shotgun guard had crawled – or been dragged – some distance from the wreck. No one else, dead or alive, was anywhere in sight.

"Jesus P. Horseshit," Jeremiah drawled.

"Apache?" Art asked nervously, looking around.

"Ain't never seen Apache do somethin' like this," Case said. He dismounted in one smooth motion, so as not to let his bulk unbalance his horse. "Well c'mon, we're here to investigate!"

The other two dismounted hesitantly, Art still looking around for Indians.

"Relax," Jeremiah chided him. "Ain't nothing but flat far as th' eye c'n see. Nowhere to hide."

"Indians can hide in plain sight. Five feet away and you'd never see them. And me without a pistol..."

"S'okeh, I got two," Jeremiah said, drawing both. There were no other men out there, red or white, Jeremiah was sure of that. But something didn't feel right. He could taste it in the air, but he couldn't quite put his finger on it, and that made him extra edgy. He for certain felt better with his iron at the ready.

Sheriff Merrick pulled open the stagecoach door and leaned inside.

And then he screamed, high-pitched, like a woman.

Stumbling backwards, he clutched his ample gut, where a bright red blossom was actively unfurling.

And he continued screaming that high-pitched scream, even though his mouth wasn't moving.

He wasn't the one screaming.

There was someone in the coach, and they'd just stabbed the sheriff in the belly.

Jeremiah let three bullets fly, two from one gun and one from the other. They threw up splinters of wood as they punched holes in the carriage. The screaming stopped.

Case dropped to his knees, and then fell backwards.

"Ah, hell," he said. Art rushed to his side.

"Girl..." the sheriff gasped. "Hold yer fire it's just a girl..." Art craned his neck to see inside the coach. Sure enough it was a girl, young – just shy of marrying age, wild-eyed, a bloody dagger gripped in both hands, business end out. Because she was hunkered down in the seat, Jeremiah's bullets had passed clean over her head. She stared at Art in terror.

"It's okeh, Miss," he said. "We're here to help."

"Stomach wound's no joke," Jeremiah said, focusing his attention on the sheriff. "We got t' get this man back to town, pronto."

"Can we lift him onto his horse?" Art asked. "Working together?"

"I shouldn't ride," Case declared. "You got to run fetch a litter or a wagon or some such. George's place is closest..."

Art was on his horse in a flash. "I'll be back!" he shouted over his shoulder as he tore off.

"Some days it don't pay to get outta bed," Case said with a forced chuckle. His hands were pressed against his stomach; blood was seeping through his fingers.

"Yer gonna be fine, Sheriff," Jeremiah said. But his mind was elsewhere.

Now wouldn't be a bad time to shin out, he realized.

He could appropriate his loaner horse and be ages away before the locals cleared up this mess and thought to come after him, if they ever even did.

Of course, they might just go ahead and lay the blame for the whole damned mess on him then, purely out of spite.

He supposed it was less trouble just to see this through. Whatever "this" was.

Okeh, then, it was settled. He was committed.

"Step on out here girl, or I'll shoot you in th' damn' face," he called out.

There was a long pause.

"Is it safe?" a hesitant voice finally responded.

"Are we safe from you, that's th' question. Ya done put down th' local law."

Carefully, she scooted out of the stage, her expensive dress riding up so that he could see her knickers. He didn't bother to avert his eyes, and once she was on solid ground she glared at him.

"You ain't no gentleman!" she spat.

"An' you ain't no lady. Set down th' knife."

"I won't neither. They might come back."

"Who's *they*?" asked Case through clenched teeth.

"Oh my goodness!" the girl exclaimed as her eyes fell on her handiwork. "Sure as I didn't mean to, I swear!" She knelt down beside Case and gently touched his shoulder. "I thought you was one of them!"

"Who's *them*?" Jeremiah repeated.

The girl looked at him like he was a damned fool.

"Them *things*," she said.

卌 ||

"HORSE CAN'T CARRY THIS TRUNK," George explained patiently. "Maybe you could *rent* the horse, and leave the trunk here as, I dunno, collateral."

"I won't be coming back this way. That's why I just want to *buy* the horse."

"It still can't carry this trunk."

"What if I drag the trunk along behind...?" The easterner trailed off, distracted by something he'd seen over George's shoulder. George turned around. There was a rider headed their way, hell-for-leather. "That fella's coming in like every Indian in the territory was on his tail. Except *nothing's* on his tail."

Now what? George groaned inwardly.

Art came tearing into the yard, drew reins as if it were an afterthought, and almost fell off his mount as it skidded and stumbled to a stop.

"That's *my* horse yer wearin' to the knuckles!" George shouted, wagging a finger at the writer.

"No time!" Art gasped. "Sheriff's hurt. Someone robbed the stage. Or shot it up, or

33

something. We need a litter or something to get him back to town."

"Damn' lumberin' fool," George grumbled, as if this were all the sheriff's fault. "I'll see what I can find."

"This the same sheriff who was so dismissive of me this morning?" the easterner chimed in. Love, that was his name, Art remembered.

"It was. But we'd appreciate it if you'd let bygones be and give us a hand."

Love shook his head and threw up his hands, somehow conveying annoyance and acquiescence in the same gesture.

"Of course I seen pictures of 'em, in books and whatnot, but I didn't know they was alive," the girl explained. "I didn't know they was dangerous."

"What... are you... on about, child?" Case asked between gritted teeth. "You... sound like someone what's... taken leave of their senses."

"I ain't no child!" the girl spat. "I'm on my way to Europe to be married!"

"Stannerds mus' be pretty low in Europe," Jeremiah scoffed. He thought for a moment "Where ya comin' *from*, anyway?" he asked.

"The Sandwich Islands." The girl folded her arms. "*You've* probably never heard of them."

When she got all uppity, her language skewed more proper, Jeremiah noticed.

"Oh my Lord, there's one of 'em now!" the girl gasped, pointing.

Jeremiah followed her gaze. There was nothing there. Just the open plain, a few leaves of grass waving in the light breeze that had kicked up. In the distance, a lonely tumbleweed drifted by.

"Ain't nothin' there, girl," Jeremiah said. Still, he readied his six-shooters. He had to admit that something for sure still didn't feel right.

"Right there!" the girl pointed. "It's coming right at us!"

"Ain't nothin' coming this way 'ceptin' that..."

Tumbleweed. There was no wind, and yet the tumbleweed had changed direction. It was coming straight towards them now. The two remaining horses seemed suddenly agitated and snorted nervously.

"What is this...?"

"Shoot it! Shoot it!" the girl shouted, grabbing fistfuls of his flannel shirt front and pressing herself up against him.

"I ain't wastin' a bullet on... on a *bush*."

"Please!" The girl was becoming hysterical.

Movement in his peripheral vision. Two more tumbleweeds to their right, headed their way. No, three.

Five from their left.

They were everywhere, he realized, concealed by tufts of grass or boulders or just plain invisible by nature because a body didn't take the time to notice them. And now they were closing in. All of them. A score, maybe more.

"Heaven's Glory..." Jeremiah whispered.

*"I didn't know they **ate** people!"* the girl sobbed.

Grabbing the girl's wrist, Jeremiah managed a single step in the direction of his horse before both mounts reared up in panic and fled in opposite directions.

"No!" he shouted. Then Jeremiah watched in slack-jawed awe as the tumbleweeds changed direction, converging on Giant, the horse that had unthinkingly bolted into their midst. Propelling themselves into Giant's path, the bushes opened up like blossoming flowers, their branches wrapping around the animal's legs and then snapping shut and holding tight. The panicked horse began running in circles, pausing to kick each leg in turn in an attempt to dislodge the things. Blood was dribbling down his legs now, from every point where one of those *things* had attached itself. Drawn by the frenzy, more tumbleweeds closed in. Squealing in pain and terror, Giant finally dropped to the ground where he kicked once, twice, and then was still. Blood pooled around the motionless animal as more and more 'weeds piled on, unfurling with a crackle like snapping twigs as they pressed flush against Giant and began to pulsate irregularly. A coppery tang filled the air.

They were feeding.

"What's happenin'???" Case demanded, struggling to sit up.

"We got to get outta here!" The girl tugged at Jeremiah. His hand was still clamped down on

her wrist, he realized.

"No – they'll run us down! C'mon!" Darting to the far side of the canted stagecoach, where the roof was nearer the ground, he made a step out of his hands and helped the girl climb on top, then scrambled up beside her. "Sheriff!" he shouted to the man below. "Yer too damn big fer me t' carry and I ain't about t' die tryin'! Git yerself inside and secure that door! I'll cover ya!" Already, two of the "tumbleweeds" were closing in. Taking careful aim with his revolvers, Jeremiah fired twice, once at each of them. His first shot missed entirely, but the second was true and the target exploded in a squealing burst of dried twigs(?) and a sickly, yellowish grue.

Sheriff Merrick was dragging himself into the stage when the surviving 'weed reached him. There was a sizable trunk strapped to the roof, and in one swift motion Jeremiah drew his Bowie knife and cut through the tie-down rope securing it, then tipped it over the side. It crushed the 'weed worrying the sheriff flat.

"What if there was stuff in that trunk we coulda *used?*" the girl scolded him.

"This ain't *Rob'son Crusoe*," Jeremiah said. "Someone don't come fer us right quick, all we'll be needin' is pen an' paper fer our last will an' testament."

They felt the stagecoach shift as Case collapsed inside. With some difficulty, he rolled over and pulled the door shut behind him. Already, a dozen more 'weeds were headed in their direction.

"Ya all right down there, Sheriff?" Jeremiah called out.

"You kiddin' me?" Case gasped.

卌 III

THE THREE RIDERS pulled up and surveyed the scene. The stage had clearly been compromised and the stage horses were inarguably dead, but there were no other mounts in sight, and the sheriff wasn't sprawled out on the ground like a stuck hog like Art had claimed, neither.

"I don't understand..." Art began.

"There's people on *top* of that stage," the easterner, Johnny Love, pointed out.

"Sure as there is," said George. "What in tarnation...?" Retrieving a pair of field glasses from one of his saddlebags, he focused on the two figures. "It's your amigo what strolled out o' the desert this morning, Art. And a girl. Purdy, too."

"But where's the sheriff?" asked Art.

George scanned the landscape in both directions.

"Don't see him nowhere, nor their horses, neither." He paused. "Wait, there's a horse. But it's dead. Looks to have been dead a while." He lowered the glasses and glared at Art. "If that fiddlehead done lost my horse..."

The man in question had spotted them now. He began waving his arms over his head and shouting something that was muffled some by distance and then plucked away entirely by the desert wind.

"What is he on about?" George asked.

"Can't make it out," said Art.

"If this is some farce you play out for all the 'greenhorns'..." Johnny Love began.

"Hush!" George said. He raised the field glasses again.

"You see something?" Art asked.

"Naw, just checking out the girl."

"What's she look like?" asked Johnny.

"Mighty purdy. Blonde. She's got pink ribbons braided in her hair. To a glance it's like she's got yella and pink hair. It's a strangely appealin' effect."

"Lemme see," said Johnny, gesturing for the glasses.

"For the love of...! **Hyah!**" Art spurred his mount and pointed it at the compromised stage, leaving the other two men choking on his dust.

"Damn it," George said. "Why's that starry-eyed fool got to be so dramatic all the time? C'mon." The two began to slowly trot after him.

The girl was ecstatic when Art pulled up next to the stage.

"You've come to rescue us!" she beamed.

"I, uh, guess I have, at that," Art blushed, tipping his hat. "Uh, Miss."

"Cotty Carmichael," the girl introduced herself.

"Harold Artemis Faust, but my friends call me..."

Jeremiah cut him off.

"Yer friends are gonna be callin' on ya at the cemetery if we don't get outta here, pronto!" Roughly scooping up the girl, he handed her down to Art. The latter made to lower her to the ground, but she clung to him and held on tight.

"Oooo, comfy," she cooed, nestling against the young man. He blushed again, redder this time.

The other two riders trotted up just at that moment.

"This looks cozy," smirked George.

"You'd best get down..." Art told Cotty.

"No and I won't! I ain't never settin' foot on the ground again until I'm safe in a proper city!" She clung to Art all the tighter.

George turned his attention to Jeremiah.

"And where's my horse, mister?"

"Yers run off. Th' other one's done been ate."

"Who ate it? The sheriff?"

"I heard that, George Bartlett!" Case shouted from inside the stage.

"There he is!" George grinned, peeping inside. "Loungin' around when there's work to be done!"

"I need a doctor and you're crackin'!" the sheriff fumed.

"Okeh, okeh, don't get your back up." George had the makings of an improvised litter strapped to the side of his horse and he climbed down and cobbled it together now. "Question is, who rides, and who gets the hernias?" he asked.

"We best move fast," Jeremiah said, somehow clambering down from the stage roof while still keeping his guns at the ready. "'Fore they come back."

"Before *who* comes back?" the easterner asked. He still sat on his horse and hadn't made a move to help.

"I don't reckon yud believe me if I told ya," Jeremiah said as he and George helped Case out of the stage and then navigated his bulk onto the litter.

"Was it Indians?" asked Love. He seemed excited at the prospect of encountering Indians.

"Weren't Indians," Jeremiah said. "They wuz... some kinda animal? Or maybe a plant? Sure as I ain't got the schoolin' t' say. But they're dangerous. Run down the sheriff's horse and nearly got us too."

"Filthy things!" Cotty interjected.

"Are you tellin' me an *animal* did all this?" George scoffed, indicating the wrecked stagecoach.

"What kind of animal?" Johnny Love asked, his eyes wide. He was fascinated.

"I plugged one o' th' critters," Jeremiah said. "There's another mashed flat under that trunk."

George strolled over, lifted the edge of the trunk, and wrinkled his nose at the dripping yellow paste he found beneath.

"Almighty," he gagged. "Looks like somebody

ate a prairie bush fer supper and then brought it back up."

"Bleedin' out, here!" Case shouted from the litter.

"All right, all right!" said George. "You, Fancy Sam," he said, indicating Love, "off the horse. You and Art are gonna be carryin' this tub o' guts." He hooked a thumb at the sheriff for emphasis.

"Now just a minute..." Love began.

"No *just a minute* about it. I supplied the horses, you can supply the manpower."

"Can you ride, Miss?" Jeremiah asked Cotty.

"I cannot." She hugged Art even tighter. "But I can hold on!"

"I'll assist this city fella with th' sheriff," Jeremiah said, finally holstering his .44s. "Lady can ride double with Art. George, you ride yer horse and lead th' other." He turned to Cotty. "We're gonna hafta slit that fancy dress o' yers up the front so's ya ain't ridin' sidesaddle," he told her.

Using the knife she still held in her hands, she did it herself, without protest.

卌 ||||

THE STRANGE PROCESSION made its way towards town, Art and Cotty in the lead, the two men carrying the sheriff behind, and George flanking the latter. The odd horse out had been tail-tied to George's mount. It was slow going, what with two of them on foot *and* carrying a man; they'd clearly be spending the next several hours in each other's company.

"Looks like we got some time to fill," George ventured after a spell, "so anyone care to explain the no doubt comical chain of events what led up to this point?"

"Them bugaboos of yours panicked the horses," Cotty said over her shoulder, "and we ran off into that ditch and broke a wheel. Then they attacked the horses, then the guard, then the other two passengers when they climbed out to 'help'. The driver, he ran off. Instead of venturing out like the others I stayed put. That's why they didn't get me."

"What are these bugaboos yer talkin' about?"

"They're real," Case wheezed from the litter.

44

"We seen 'em."

"Look fer all the world like tumblin' scrub weeds," Jeremiah nodded, "but then they come after ya."

"I ain't never heard of no such. Yer all loco."

"They're *Menehune*," Cotty said, so quietly that only Art could hear her. "Except evil."

"What's that?" asked Art.

"The small people," she whispered. "In Hawai'i they're kind and helpful. Here they must be evil."

"You know what I think?" George continued. "I think y'all was set upon by a herd of warrior rabbits!" He laughed heartily at his own joke.

"What's a warrior rabbit?" asked Johnny.

"Why, a warrior rabbit is a sort of jackrabbit, 'cept it's got horns like a longhorn steer. They can imitate the human voice, and sometimes, late at night, they'll do just that and lure a body off into the dark so's they can dry gulch 'em and eat their soft parts."

"Wow!" Johnny said breathlessly.

"He's kiddin' ya, Mister," Jeremiah said.

"And that's no story to tell when a lady's present!" Art chimed in. Did Cotty hold on just a little tighter after he said that? He thought so.

"So what happened to the sheriff?" George asked.

"Girl stuck me," Case wheezed. "Accidental-like."

"If that's yer story, girl, stick to it," George told Cotty.

It was dusk by the time Outskirts loomed up

out of the desert. Spurring his horse, Art rode ahead to inform Doc Hathaway that they were coming. Jeremiah had a distinct sensation of *déjà vu*. How many bodies was he going to help carry in out of the desert? Outskirts, Arizona, did not appear to be a healthy place to be.

"Soon as you get me settled, I want y'all t' organize a hunt," the sheriff wheezed. "Round up as many as'll participate. First light of day, I want them tumblin' monstrosities run to ground. We'll put a bounty on 'em – a dollar per."

"Folks are likely to shoot up the whole territory," George countered. "You sure about this, Sheriff?"

"They're a menace."

"They're a figment of the imagination, ya ask me."

"I seen 'em too," Jeremiah reminded him.

"And who *are* you, anyway?" George asked irritably. "You come strollin' into town and suddenly there's bodies everywhere!"

"Lookin' to join that exclusive group?" Jeremiah asked offhandedly.

"Best not..."

"Look," Johnny Love happily interrupted, "that Art fellow's coming back!"

He was, tearing across the scrub at full speed. Cotty, who was still with him, was hanging on for dear life.

"Doc's gone!" he shouted before he even reached them.

"Ah, hellcakes," Case groaned.

"Where would he have gone off to this time o' day?" George asked out loud

"I don't think he *went* anyplace," Art gasped as he pulled up. "He's just gone. *Everybody* is gone."

卌 卌

IT WAS TRUE. The street was deserted. There was a checkerboard set up on an upturned barrel on the plankboard sidewalk in front of the pharmacy, but no one was playing. The saloon was deserted, although a couple of drinks had been set up and waited patiently on the bar. Art dismounted and ran first to one residence, then the next, pounding on each door with the flat of his hand. No one was home. Outskirts had become a ghost town before its time.

"They ate 'em," Cotty said. She was still straddling the horse, holding onto the saddle pommel for dear life. "They ate the whole town."

"Somebody help that girl down," George said. Art did the honors, and then George secured all three mounts to the nearest hitching post.

"If they ate ever'body, there'd be signs," Jeremiah said.

"Maybe everyone ran off?" Art suggested.

"Inta the desert? When there's places here to hole up an' fortify?" Jeremiah shook his head. "No, it don't make no sense."

48

"Can we *please* set this man down?" Johnny groaned. "My arms are going numb!"

"In the pharmacy," Art said, leading the way. Heddy would have been dismayed that they once again carried the body through her drawing room. Sweeping the skeleton from earlier onto the floor, they carefully lifted Sheriff Merrick onto the examination table.

"How you holdin' up?" George asked him as he lit the wall lamp with a match. It was clear that there was a lot more blood than they'd realized – his shirt and the litter were soaked through. Cotty averted her eyes and Art dutifully put his arm around her shoulders and led her outside.

"Cold..." Case mumbled.

"What should we do?" Johnny asked.

"Sterilize it an' sew 'im up," Jeremiah said. "But knowin' *what* an' knowin' *how* are vastly diff'rent things."

"Fancy Pants," George said, addressing Johnny, "run get me a bottle from the saloon. Strongest stuff they got." The easterner was clearly annoyed but did as he was asked.

"Doc... has... sterilizin' alcohol... right here... in the pharmacy," Case said. His voice was barely a whisper now.

"The bottle's for me," George said. "I'm gonna try my hand at sewin' you up, Sheriff, and I ain't about to attempt that feat sober."

"Ya ever perform surg'ry before?" Jeremiah asked.

"Delivered a colt once," George said. Locating

a bottle labeled "Alcohol", George splashed a generous amount of its contents on the wound. Only then did he realize that he should've removed the sheriff's shirt first.

"Ferget it," Jeremiah said as George cut the bloody, alcohol-soaked shirt away with his knife.

"I can do this," George said.

"Ya c'n raise th' dead?" Jeremiah asked. The sheriff's chest was no longer rising and falling.

"Damn it," said George. He gripped the side of the table and took a deep breath.

"He musta been bleedin' on th' inside. Nothin' you could do."

"I could shoot that stab-happy tart in the belly."

"Won't solve nothin'."

"You got an answer fer everything, don't ya?" George snapped, storming out of the room.

Jeremiah expected to walk outside into a confrontation, but George was standing apart from the others, his back to them, staring at the sky. A few stars were already out, and they twinkled impassively. George rolled a quirley, lit it, and inhaled the smoke slowly and deliberately. Cotty still clung to Art. The latter had no idea what to do with his own arms, and they hung awkwardly at his side. Johnny Love, who had returned, quietly opened and drank from the bottle he'd fetched. The horses stamped nervously.

"It's all too peculiar fer me," George said after

a long time. He still stared at the sky. The stars were out in full force now, and the last red smears of the sunset were disappearing below the horizon.

"We need to fetch the Army," Love said. He took another swallow from his appropriated bottle.

"Let's do that! Right now!" Cotty said.

"No," Jeremiah said. "Not 'til mornin'. We ride out now, horse'll step on a prairie dog hole, or somethin'll come up at us outta the dark. We'll wait 'til we got some proper light."

"Aw, hellbiscuits!" George said. "My horses! I got to go out there and check on 'em!"

"That doesn't strike me as a good idea, George," Art said.

"Good idea or no, we're gonna need at least one more of them horses."

Everyone looked around. Five of them, three horses.

"How good are you with them irons, fella?" George asked Jeremiah.

"Good enough."

"I'm no slouch either," Love broke in.

"That thing looks like it ain't never even been fired," George said, indicating Love's shiny Model 3.

Faster than anyone's eyes could follow, Johnny Love quick-drew the piece and fired off a round. The sound was like a cannon in the empty street. Grinning, he re-holstered the weapon.

"Hope nobody was in the path o' that bullet,"

George said, making a show of being unimpressed.

"What's it take, huh?" Love said defensively. He took a step towards George.

"Alright," Jeremiah said, holding up his hands. "No need t' scrap amongst ourselves. Me an' Mr. Love here will go fer the horses. On foot. That way we c'n bring back two."

"Like spit!" said George. "Who's to say you won't jest run off with 'em?"

George had a good point, especially as that was, indeed, Jeremiah's plan.

"Fine," he acquiesced, "you an' me, then."

George nodded. He located a lantern and a shotgun, lit the former and loaded the latter.

"Th' rest y'all stay here, at th' pharmacy," Jeremiah said. "This shouldn't take us more'n what, half an hour?"

"If that," George nodded.

"And if you're not back in half an hour?" Cotty asked.

"Shoot yerselves," Jeremiah said.

卌 卌 |

JOHNNY AND ART secured the pharmacy door from the inside and then pushed a heavy cabinet up against it for good measure. Satisfied, Johnny retrieved his bottle and started working on it again.

"You'd best lay off that," Cotty chastised him. "What if we need your shootin' skills?"

"I'm sure your boyfriend will step up to protect you," Love said, indicating Art.

"He ain't my boyfriend! I'm engaged to be *married!* And in case you didn't notice, he ain't even wearin' a gun!"

"Say, you aren't," Love noted. "I thought everyone in the wild, woolly west owned a handgun."

"I do own one," Art said, a bit defensively. "I just don't carry it. It's in a strongbox in my room, across the street."

"Great place for it," Cotty scoffed.

"I'm a *writer*. What's a writer got to constantly be heeled for?"

"Critics?" Love suggested, then laughed at his

own joke.

Everyone was quiet for a moment.

"What's happening?" Cotty finally ventured. "Where is everyone?"

Art shook his head.

"I don't know. I just..."

"...don't know. I ain't *never* seen their like."

"Well I'll believe it when I see it with my own two," George said. The rising moon cast pitiful little light, but the lantern threw enough for them to see where they were going. It helped that George had taken this route to and from town hundreds of times over the years.

"They're like nothin' I ever seen. Like somethin' that jest dropped out o' th' sky," Jeremiah went on. He was trying to sort this out in his own head, and didn't really care if George believed him or not.

"Maybe they're from the moon," George suggested. "I heard tell that there's people up there, of a sort, and all manner of beasts and critters mankind ain't never seen before. Maybe some of 'em, I dunno, fell off or somethin'."

They both stole a glance at the rising satellite.

"Sounds like yer startin' t' believe me," Jeremiah smiled.

"Easy to believe anything out here in the dark," George said.

There was a rustling sound to their left, accompanied by a peripheral sense of motion. Both men froze.

"Ya hear that?" Jeremiah whispered.

"That I did." They drew their firearms.

A chill night-desert wind suddenly kicked up, powerful enough to set their clothes flapping. Jeremiah had to snatch his hat out of the air as it almost sailed away.

"Can't hear, can't see. I'm not likin' this," he groused.

The rustling again, to their right. George spun on it and almost fired, but managed to restrain himself. "Come out!" he shouted into the darkness. "We hear ya!"

Nothing.

"This is wrackin' every nerve I got," Jeremiah said. "An' then some."

Another gust of wind. The light from the lantern danced wildly, creating confusing shadows.

"There!" said George, aiming the shotgun. Something was tumbling by just at the outer edge of their vision.

"Wait!" said Jeremiah. Clearing leather in the blink of an eye the gunfighter fired once, hitting the thing square, the force of the bullet propelling it out of sight into the darkness.

"You got it!" Holding the lantern high, they approached the place where they last saw the thing.

"Where'd it go?" Jeremiah asked, looking around.

"There," George pointed at a vague shape bounding away from them in the darkness, having again been taken by the wind. It was a tumbleweed. Just an ordinary, everyday tumbleweed. "Damn' if you didn't have me believin'..."

He started screaming. Spinning, flailing, he fell to the ground as scores of dry, branch-like tendrils wrapped around his leg. Gripping the shotgun in both hands, he started mashing his assailant with the stock, hollering all the while, a mixture of fear and anger. As he pummeled the thing pieces cracked and broke off with the sound of dry, snapping twigs. "It's bitin' me! It's bitin' me!" he howled.

Ducking the business end of the shotgun, Jeremiah stepped in, plunged his .44 into the attacking mass, and fired. "Ah, shit!" George cried out. Powder burns on his leg, no doubt. But the thing had been dislodged, and, remaining open like a flower in bloom, it fell to the ground and was still.

Jeremiah approached it carefully.

There was a *face* at the center of it. And it wasn't dead. It thrashed and mewed pitifully as a dirty, yellow ichor pumped sluggishly out of the place where the bullet had gone through. It had eight eyes – two big ones surrounded by six smaller ones – all of them as smooth and black as a pond at midnight. Its mouth was a vicious black beak, like a parrot's, the tip of it glistening in the moonlight with a smear of George's blood. Jeremiah couldn't shake the impression that he was a looking at a spider – the biggest, weirdest spider he had ever seen. But it wasn't no spider, because spiders didn't have a hide made out of dried branches that doubled as grippy-grabby appendages. George limped over and joined him just as the thing shuddered in its final death throe and then, popping and crackling, closed up like a flower going to sleep. Despite the impenetrable blackness of its eyes, Jeremiah could've sworn that he saw a sort of light go out of them as the thing expired. Probably just a trick of the moonlight, or the flickering lantern that had been dropped to the ground but hadn't gone out.

"Jesus and all his saints..." George whispered.

"C'n ya walk?" Jeremiah asked.

"Ain't nothin'," George said, shifting his weight from one leg to the other. "But it burns." His trousers were torn and smeared with gore, but he didn't appear to be bleeding profusely.

"Go back?" Jeremiah asked.

"Like hell. We're more'n halfway there."

$$\text{IIII IIII II}$$

SEVEN MINUTES LATER they reached the edge of George's property. He was limping now, favoring his injured leg, but this didn't stop him from increasing his gait, rushing into the stable to check on his beloved horses.

Holding the lantern high, he groaned audibly.

The majority of the horses weren't dead, but at first glance they appeared to be. They lay on their sides in their individual stalls, breathing slowly and methodically, in no way reacting when George approached them, spoke to them, gently patted a favorite mare on the side. Their flesh was cold – not *dead* cold, but sick cold, as if they had a mysterious opposite-fever that made them cool to the touch rather than warm. The sole exception was George's prize stallion. This animal was quite dead – frozen solid, flakes of frost visible around its nostrils and at its extremities. To the touch it felt less like a frozen corpse than an exceptionally lifelike statue, carved from a chunk of glacier.

"What done this?" George asked no one in

particular. "What *coulda* done this?"

Jeremiah shook his head. It was sheer madness.

"I got to put 'em out of their misery," George said. There was a hitch in his voice.

"Why don't ya tend t' that leg, lemme take care'a this?" Jeremiah said.

George shook his head no, emphatically, but then handed the shotgun over and gimped outside without another word. Jeremiah took no joy in the task, but performed it quickly and efficiently. Only the prize stallion gave him pause. It seemed pointless, and yet something told him that he had to see to this animal, too. Trusting his gut, he loaded a final cartridge and held the shotgun up to the stallion's head. It was, indeed, frozen solid, clean through, and when he pulled the trigger its head shattered like a block of ice.

"It's dun," he said, joining George outside. The latter had plopped down on the ground and was carefully cutting the right leg of his trousers and union suit off with a knife. His injured leg had swollen up something fierce, and the skin had taken on a crimson tint so red that it almost glowed.

"Poison, I'm thinkin'," George said matter-of-factly. He was quiet for a moment that seemed to stretch on forever. Producing a pouch of tobacco from a pocket, he slowly rolled a quirley, struck a match, lit it, and inhaled the smoke deeply.

"Those wasn't my horses," he finally said. "I

know what yer thinkin', but I knowed each of them animals like they was my own children, and it wasn't them. Not the *real* them. It's like... they was there, but what made them *them* was gone. Like someone come and took their... I dunno..." he grasped for the word "...their *essence* and just left the shell behind." He stared off into the desert. "I suppose I sound plumb crazy."

Maybe we're all gone crazy, Jeremiah thought

What he said was, "C'n ya walk on that leg?"

"Hurts, but yeah. Though I'm thinkin' mebbe we hunker down in the house 'til dawn. Be nice, on the walk back, to act'lly be able to see anything what's comin' after us."

Jeremiah nodded. Somewhere, a lone coyote cried out mournfully, only to be cut off with a sudden yelp, as if something bigger and hungrier had unexpectedly grabbed it.

The two men hurried inside.

卌 卌 |||

"THEY'RE DEAD," Johnny said, gesturing with his half-empty bottle. "Dead or run off. Which suits us just fine. Three people, three horses. First crack of day we can... what is it you cowpunchers say? *...light a suck* for parts not here."

"It's light a *shuck*," Art corrected him. He was staring out the pharmacy window, squinting into the darkness.

"An' it's parts *unknown*," Cotty added.

"But they're *not* unknown," Johnny said. "If we know where we're going then it's not parts *unknown*. It's just... parts."

"You're drunk!"

He held the bottle out to her.

"You're welcome to join me," he said.

"I think not."

"Well don't blame me for your bad decisions later," he shrugged, taking another sip.

"Harold, do something!" Cotty demanded, addressing Art by his first name.

"Yeah, *Harold*, do something!" Johnny laughed.

61

"Shush! I think I see something!" Art said.

"Close your *eyes*, I think he *hears* something!" Johnny told Cotty, then laughed uproariously.

"It's them! I can see their lantern!" He rushed to the door and began sliding the heavy cabinet aside. Cotty went to the window herself, nudged the curtain aside, and peeped out.

"A bunch of lanterns," she said. "It's a whole mess of folks."

"The Cavalry has arrived!" Johnny exclaimed. He took a celebratory drink.

"It's not the Cavalry," Cotty said. "They're on foot."

"Budget cuts?" Johnny suggested. Art stopped struggling with the cabinet and both men joined her at the window.

The lights, dozens of them now, drew closer, swaying, wavering. As they approached they took form; not lanterns, but figures, pale blue and flickering. Transparent people, each face a mask of misery and woe, trudging dutifully down Outskirts' main street, wailing lamentations so devoid of hope that it brought tears to Art's eyes and chilled him to the bone. "No..." Johnny whispered, backing away from the window. Cotty gasped and clung to Art, but somehow she couldn't look away as the procession passed slowly by, a hundred spirits or more, wailing in anguish, weeping uncontrollably, rending their ethereal garments.

And then one of them saw her.

For Cotty, everything ceased to exist. There

were only the eyes, all-encompassing. For the merest instant it was as if she were one with the owner of those eyes, as if they were the same being. She shared its pain, its confusion, its terror... and most of all the knowledge that *They* were coming.

They.

Cotty screamed, and the spell was broken.

Art and Johnny both tensed up, expecting every spectral head to turn in their direction now, but the procession continued on its way, and less than a minute later it was lost from sight.

Johnny was examining the bottle in his hand.

"I've heard of seeing snakes in your boots, and being followed by pink giraffes, but I ain't never heard of anything like that," he said quietly.

"They're coming," Cotty said, staring off into the middle distance. "This is only the beginning."

"Who's coming?" Art asked.

"Them that's hunting 'em. Hunting the damned."

"The damned?" Art repeated. The girl sounded as though she'd taken leave of her senses.

"Midnight," she said, and then swooned. Had this been a dime novel, Art would have caught her, deftly, in his arms. As it was she simply collapsed to the wooden floor.

Johnny surreptitiously fished out his pocket watch and noted the time.

It was half past ten.

卌 卌 IIII

"YA HEAR THAT?" George asked from the chesterfield. His leg, propped up on a wooden chair so that it was parallel to the floor, had swollen to the point where he couldn't bend it at the knee.

"That leg o' yers looks like one o' them blood sausages," Jeremiah noted.

"Never mind that. *Listen.*"

Jeremiah listened. Outside the wind was picking up, but beneath it he could hear a sort of rustling, first on one side of the house, then the other.

"They know we're in here," George said.

"Let 'em know. Nothin' they c'n do about it 'lessin they can pass thru walls."

"An' if they can?"

Jeremiah held up one of his revolvers.

"I'll pass lead thru *them.*"

George studied Jeremiah for several seconds.

"Who are you, anyway, Mister?" he finally asked. "What brung you to a tiny burg like Outskirts sans horse, sans money, and sans the good sense to just pass right on through?"

"Well, if ya must know, I paid th' inevitable price o' trusting a man name o' Tony Grillcakes."

"Grillcakes? Now that sounds like a made-up name if I *ever* heard one."

"Likely is. Might say he wuz my business partner, but th' ennerprise went sour and, well, he sent some fellas t' collect somethin' he felt wuz due and I felt wuzn't. Fed one o' them fellas a lead breakfast. Th' other chased me halfway 'cross th' territory 'fore I finally shook 'im."

"Somethin' tells me this enterprise of yers wasn't exactly on the up-'n'-up."

"Mebbe so." Jeremiah's tone was dismissive.

There was a sudden change in the atmosphere of the room, a dramatic drop in pressure.

"What the jackrabbit hell...?" George began.

The air all around them seemed to retreat, like the drawback before a tsunami. Then, a low, drawn-out blast, echoing across the desert, as if Gabriel himself had finally seen fit to step down from Heaven and let loose on his famous horn. Outside, the desert creatures for miles around fled in all directions, blind with panic but unsure which direction to run. The note faded slowly, and in the utter silence that followed the temperature fell like it was dropped off a cliff, a full twenty degrees in half as many minutes. Jeremiah could see his breath.

"What is happenin'?" Jeremiah wondered out loud.

"I don't know," George said. "I don't know."

"I know," Cotty deadpanned. Art gave her another sip of water.

"Sure is cold all of a sudden," Johnny said, wrapping his arms around himself.

"Know what?" Art asked Cotty, ignoring the easterner.

"I know what *he* knew. The spirit. He showed me in his eyes." She looked Art in the eyes now, her face desperate and wild, grabbing a handful of his shirtfront and shrieking. *"They're coming! The Raging Host! We shouldn't **be** here!"*

"Raging Host?" Johnny asked. "Like if you upset someone who's invited you to a dinner party?"

"The Host! The Host! The Fair Folk! They're coming, coming to hunt the damned!"

"You said that already," Johnny said. He wished he had some more whiskey to dip into, but he didn't cotton to the idea of going across the street to the saloon to get another bottle.

"Cotty, please," Art held her shoulders firmly. "Who are the damned?"

"Not me, I'm a saint," said Johnny. Unconsciously, he made the sign of the cross, even though he hadn't been to Mass since he was a child.

"Them that just passed us by. The spirits. They've been let loose an' given a head start. It's more..." she swallowed "...*sporting* that way."

"Let loose from where?" Art swallowed nervously. "H-Hell?"

"She's crazy as a loon," Johnny said.

"No, not Hell," Cotty said. "They're... *on loan.* Hell's done loaned them to the Fair Folk to hunt for sport." Her voice fell to a whisper. "If they get away, if they evade the hunt 'til dawn, they get to go back to Hell."

"That doesn't sound like much of an incentive," Johnny said.

"Oh but it is," Cotty assured him. "Because being caught by the Fair Folk is *so much worse.*"

She buried her face in her hands and wept.

Jeremiah helped George to his feet.

"C'n ya walk?" he asked.

"In a manner of speakin'," George said, taking a few stiff-legged steps.

A howl swept across the desert. Beneath the ever-increasing wind, Jeremiah thought he heard the baying of hounds.

"Whatever's happ'nin', I wanna be far, far away when it does. We make fer town as fast as yer leg'll allow, and then we're ridin' outta here, light or no light."

George shook his head.

"I don't want one of my horses carryin' two men any considerable distance. It's hell on their legs an' innards."

"As Cath'rine th' Great might say, fuck yer horses. We got men need savin'. If ya think someone needs t' stay behind, feel free t' volunteer."

George's only response was to secure his shotgun beneath his arm, throw open the door, and, lantern held high, step out into the storm.

卌 卌 卌

THE AIR STANK of ozone, and lighting jackknifed across the sky in jagged thrusts that were visible even through the maelstrom of swirling dust. Heads down, the two men began to trudge towards town, George in the lead, Jeremiah behind. *At least them rollin' spider-scrubs won't be able t' creep up on us,* Jeremiah thought to himself. With any luck, the wind would carry them off entirely and deposit them somewhere on the rarefied side of the Mississippi.

It was impossible to speak without yelling, so they simply walked, and this gave Jeremiah time to think.

Where *did* those miserable, unnatural things come from? *Did* they just fall out of the sky? But if that were so, why hadn't it ever happened before? More likely, they'd been living in some desert hidey-hole since forever, and, by whatever coincidence, this just happened to be the first time folks had encountered them.

Or maybe not the first time. Maybe just the first time folks had encountered them and lived

69

to tell the tale.

And even the living to tell the tale part wasn't certain, yet.

So where was their hidey-hole? Some lost valley full of monsters from the dim past, like them "dinosaurs" whose dusty old bones were always making the papers?

It was beginning to rain. Not a true rain, not yet, but scattered, plump drops that were cold as ice and promised many more to come.

The door.

He'd seen a door, in the wall of that canyon.

But no, he hadn't, not really. He'd just imagined it.

But what if he hadn't?

The horses were skittish and agitated, stamping and balking at Art's touch. Fat, ice-cold drops of rain began to fall lazily around them.

"We can't ride in this," Art frowned. "This storm's gonna hit hard."

"We can't stay!" Cotty insisted. "They took everyone else so's to clear their hunting ground! We shouldn't *be* here!"

Lightning arced across the sky, followed by a low rumble of thunder.

Art approached the strawberry roan, the least anxious of the three horses. Gently, he stroked its cheek, speaking to it softly. When he had quieted it down he took it by the reins and unhitched it.

"We'll stable the horses in the saloon," he said. "I think..."

A ululating, baleful howl filled the air, seeming to come from everywhere at once. The roan, panicking, reared up and nearly kicked Art in the head as its feet churned the air. Trumpeting in terror, it bolted just as the rain came, charging blindly through the brief, resultant curtain of swirling sand and water onto the sidewalk where it stumbled and crashed-ran headfirst through the glass display window fronting the general store. Crashing to the floor, it flailed about, kicking wildly, unintentionally destroying everything within reach, before letting out a single, horrific squeal of intermingled pain and terror. Then it was still.

The other two horses lost their minds. One tore the post it was hitched to right out of the ground and galloped off, dragging the post behind. The other deftly pulled itself loose and turned on them, rearing and kicking as they dove for cover. Then it, too, raced off into the storm.

"No! No!" Cotty wailed. Johnny cleared leather and fired two shots at the retreating form of the second horse.

"What the fool hell are you doing?!" Art shouted.

"Damned bastard almost killed us!" Johnny snarled.

The three of them were soaked now, smeared head to toe with mud. Cotty was screaming uncontrollably. *"Save me, oh somebody save me!!!"* she shrieked to no one in particular. Art went to her, pulled her to her feet. "They'll *hurt* us," she babbled, clinging to him. "Oh how they'll hurt us and they'll *like* it..."

"Something's coming!" Johnny interrupted.

Something was. A dim light, bobbling towards them in the distance, just visible through the wavering sheets of rain.

Johnny raised his fancy gun and fired.

An instant later the bobbing light returned fire, the bullet zipping by so close to Cotty that she felt its passage, a hot streak across her left cheek. She squeaked and sensibly dropped to the ground, taking Art with her.

"Who's there?!" Johnny shouted belatedly.

"Stop shootin', you chucklehead!" George's voice answered.

"Put that gun away before you *kill* somebody!" Cotty hissed from the mud. Nearly dying had apparently cleared her head.

"Well, you two are a sight for sore ones," Art said as the two men approached. George was favoring one of his legs.

"Where's the horses?" Johnny asked.

"Might ask you the same thing," George growled.

"Run off because of the storm," Art said. "I'm sorry."

"It's not the storm," Cotty said. "They know what's coming. They can sense it."

"Whut is she...?" Jeremiah began. George cut him off.

"Can we *please* get in outta the rain?" he asked.

卌 卌 卌 |

THEY LAY GEORGE carefully on the floor of the pharmacy. The skin of his infected leg, bright red and taut, was splitting now in several places. Cotty located several lengths of bandage and began to wrap it in an attempt to stanch the bleeding.

Outside the wind howled, accompanied by something else.

"What happened to him?" Art asked Jeremiah.

"I'm right here," George interjected. "Not dead yet."

"One o' them 'weeds got 'im. Poison, I'd venture. I seen it up close, all opened-up like, an' I ain't no etty-mologist but I'd swear I wuz lookin' at a gigantic bug."

"*Entomologist*," Art corrected him automatically. Only later did he wonder where a man like Jeremiah picked up the word *etymologist* in the first place.

"Those things are the least of our problems," Cotty said as she tightened George's dressing. She seemed almost preternaturally focused on

73

the task, as if it were grounding her. "We have to get out of here! You all heard the horn! You can hear the hounds now, if you listen!"

Jeremiah looked at Art questioningly.

"We saw a whole mess of spooks," he explained. "Ghosts, just strolling down Main Street like they owned the place."

"One of them put the evil eye on Miss Cotty here," Johnny added.

"It weren't the evil eye!" she snapped. "I think... I think he was tryin' to *warn* me. Us."

"Warn you about what?" George asked.

"The Fair Folk." She whispered it, as if fearful that the entities in question would hear her.

"What's that?" asked Jeremiah.

"They're *old*," Cotty said, her voice so low the men had to strain to hear it. "Their kind is so much older than human folk. A used-up people, nearing the end. And it's made them *depraved*. They're sick inside. And oh how they resent us, because we're *young*. They're here to hunt them spirits we saw. They come through a... a door between their world and ours. They're mainly interested in the spirits, but if we get in their way, if we see them, they'll take us, too, take us back with them."

A door between worlds.

Jeremiah pondered this.

A door.

"Are you telling us these 'Fair Folk' snatched everyone in town?" George asked, incredulous.

Cotty nodded.

"Yer as loco as you are beautiful," he concluded.

"There's a precedent for this," Art said.

"The beautiful ones is always crazy," George agreed.

"No, what she said. Roanoke."

Everyone just stared at him. He sighed.

"*Roanoke* was one of the first English settlements in the New World, but the entire colony, to the man, disappeared one day without a trace."

"So you think these 'Fair Folk' got 'em?" George frowned.

"It's as good an explanation as any."

"I'd question that statement."

"I seen it," Jeremiah said.

"What?" asked Art.

"Yer door, young lady," he clarified, addressing Cotty. "I think I *seen* it."

卌 卌 卌 ||

"THINK OF THIS 'DOOR' AS THE DOOR TO YOUR HOUSE," Art said. "You go in and out as you please, maybe locking it behind you, maybe not. But then say someone else opens it, or you do but you're in a hurry and forget to close it behind you. Now any manner of critter can pass through. Mice, maybe, or an unusually intrepid coyote..."

"Or giant, tumblin' sagebrush spiders," Jeremiah finished for him.

"Exactly!" Art beamed.

"So yer sayin' that these Freaky-Folk left their door open and let their equiv'lant of prairie mice into our house?" George asked.

"Or out of their house. The analogy kind of breaks down at this point, but you get the idea."

"But that's th' least our problems iff'n what th' young lady here sez is true." Jeremiah drew each of his revolvers in turn, spun the cylinder, made sure every chamber was loaded.

"We all saw the spirits, that's a fact," said Art. Johnny nodded in agreement.

"Well," said Jeremiah, "it seems t' me th' thing

t' do is close that door."

"They'll likely just open it again. I'm guessing they've been going in and out of it for years."

"Centuries," Cotty declared.

"Then we close it permanent-like. Bring th' whole canyon down on it."

"And how do you propose we do that?" Johnny asked. The briefest of grins flickered across Jeremiah's face.

"Where do y'all keep yer dynamite?"

The rain had stopped, and the wind had died down to nothing, an eerie silence descending in their wake. A flash of translucent-blue impressed itself upon Jeremiah's peripheral vision and he turned just in time to see something roughly the size of a man flit across the far end of the street and through an open doorway.

"Didja see that?" he asked George, one hand dropping to the butt of a gun.

"Nope," George said.

Lantern held high, he gimped across the street and into the general store, and Jeremiah followed. Stepping around the body of the unfortunate horse, they made their way to the back, where a small storage area was stacked with crates.

"A couple easterners had it brung in," George explained. "They was convinced that all they had to do was wander around the countryside fer a spell and they'd fall ass-over-bracket into a silver mine. Well, one of 'em fell, all right – right off the top of a thirty-foot rise. Broke both legs and a shoulder besides. His partner shipped him back east and stuck it out for a couple more weeks, but he run out of funds soon enough and that was the end of that."

"Lucky break fer us," Jeremiah said.

"Look fer one that says 'Apricots'."

"'Apricots'?" Jeremiah pronounced the i like a hard e.

"Sheriff told Nash – he's what owns this place – to burn that dynamite straight away, because he knew the fool would stash it in a corner somewhere and ferget about it until it started sweatin' and blew the place sky-high. Course, that's exac'ly what he did."

"Here," said Jeremiah. He'd found it, on the floor, pushed against the back wall.

"Okeh," George said. He tried to crouch, but his swollen leg wouldn't have it so he simply sat down next to the crate instead. "You know dynamite?" he asked Jeremiah.

"Not as such."

George frowned. Some idiot had driven two nails through the loose-fit lid to hold it on.

"Damn, hell, and all the saints besides. Find me a pry bar."

Jeremiah found one. Slowly, delicately, George worked it under each nail, carefully pulling them out, the wood protesting loudly. Then he gently lifted the lid and looked inside. The sticks neatly stacked inside were lightly coated with a yellowish, powdery crust.

"This is what we call far from optimal," George whispered.

"C'n we move it?" Jeremiah asked. Without realizing it, he'd lowered his voice too.

"We can *do* anything we want. Do we survive the experience, *that's* the question." He shook his head. "Maybe it's best we just skedaddle. Let the Army handle this..."

There was an unearthly ululation from just outside, followed by a second scream – Cotty's – and then the sound of gunfire.

"Ah, hell, now what?"

卌 卌 卌 |||

GUNS DRAWN, Jeremiah burst out of the general store... and froze. The scene outside left him dizzy with incomprehension, suddenly nostalgic for the relative rationality of mere ghosts.

A great grey hound, half again the size of a large horse, crouched in the middle of the street, inarguably substantial and yet somehow holding one of the discarnate spirits the others had described firmly in its slavering jaws. The ghost was writhing and mewing in terror, but the hound's attention was less on it and more on Johnny, who had stepped out of the pharmacy and was firing his Smith & Wesson at it. Ineffectually, as it turned out, because while the thing smarted as each bullet struck, the damage they were doing appeared to be minimal. Making a split-second decision, Jeremiah darted back into the store, scooped up a single crusty stick of dynamite over George's terrified protestations, and, returning, hurled it at the beast, only for the stick to bounce harmlessly off its hide and fall to the street. Curious, the hound – the struggling

80

ghost still gripped in its jaws – lowered its head to sniff this strange new object. It nudged the stick with its nose.

And that's when it exploded, reducing the animal's head and forequarters to a geyser of bone particulate and steaming meat.

The hound's remains collapsed to the street amidst a brief shower of grue and ectoplasm, the latter all that remained of its erstwhile victim.

It registered that Cotty was still screaming, but a moment later she stopped.

"So you found the dynamite?" Johnny asked.

"There's another one!" Art shouted, pointing to the far end of the street. "That's three since we been out here!" The spirit he was referring to flitted nervously along the sidewalk a piece before disappearing into an alley.

"This is doubtless th' best place t' hide for miles around. Endless nooks an' crannies..." Jeremiah said, clearly disinterested. He was oh-so-carefully placing the crate of dynamite on the back of a toy pull-wagon that had belonged to Doc Hathaway's children. The word *Express* was written in stylized script down the wagon's side. The others kept a fair distance as he performed this action, aside from Johnny, who hovered over him, supervising.

"They're drawing the Host right to us!" Cotty groaned. "We *have* to get out of here!"

"We will an' we are," Jeremiah nodded. "Y'all c'n strike out in any direction ya see fit. Me, I aim t' put an end t' this."

"I think it'd be a lot safer of we stuck together," Art said.

"Likely so. Those that agree, folly me."

Art briefly wondered if this was intentional wordplay, or just another example of Jeremiah's cadence.

George shook his head.

"No chance I can hobble all the way to the canyon on this leg," he said. It did, indeed, look worse.

"Hunker down in th' pharmacy, then," Jeremiah said. "If we don't blow ourselves up or get eaten, we'll be back fer ya."

George nodded, confirmed that his shotgun was loaded, and then painfully limped into not the pharmacy, but the saloon.

They never saw him again.

卌 卌 卌 ||||

JOHNNY AND ART, who had retrieved his pistol from his room, covered the motley procession, while Cotty, a lantern in each hand, led the way. All three kept their distance from Jeremiah, who was pulling the little toy wagon. The going was painfully slow, and Art bit his lower lip every time the wagon tilted slightly or navigated even the most inconsequential incline. His lip was soon bloody.

They'd been walking for almost an hour when Johnny approached Art and drew his attention to the glimmering blue shape that was trailing them.

"Been back there for several minutes now," he said. "It's not coming any closer but it's definitely following us."

Art frowned.

"We need to shoo it off before it draws attention to us," he said.

"How do you shoo off a ghost?" Even as he asked, Johnny raised his pistol and aimed at it.

"That won't work!" Art chastised him.

"You sure?" Johnny asked.

"Well, no. But even if it did, as likely the noise would draw attention to us too."

"What's goin' on back there?" Jeremiah stage whispered. His voice carried a surprising distance in the desert night.

"We've picked up a tail," Johnny said.

"Maybe it thinks we can help it," Art suggested. "'Any port in a storm,' and all that?"

Jeremiah reflected on this for a moment.

"Mebbe that goes both ways." He addressed Cotty. "Ya say ya c'n *talk* t' it, girl?"

"My name isn't *girl*," Cotty huffed, crossing her arms.

"We ain't discussin' universal suffrage, Miss. C'n you communicate with it, or not?"

"I'm afraid," she said simply, wringing her hands.

"I'll go with you," Art said, gently touching her arm.

"Okeh," she nodded.

Taking her hand, Art led Cotty towards the flickering blue figure. As they neared it, it suddenly jerked up and back into the air, as if tugged by an invisible string. Now safely out of reach, it hovered, luminescent and wavering, its eyes following their approach. It was male, Art realized, or had been in life. Its bodily form was a rippling tatter that gave the impression of a torn and battered cloak, constantly moving in some unfelt wind. The visage peering out of that tatter radiated hate, hate so powerful that Art could taste it in his mouth, like a dirty silver dollar.

"H-hello?" Cotty stammered.

The thing appeared to study her, its eyes crawling up and down her form. Slowly, slowly, it settled back to earth. Art's stomach did a somersault as two appendages – arms – cautiously reached out to them.

"Does it want a hug?" Johnny whispered to Jeremiah.

"Quiet."

"Maybe..." She swallowed nervously. "Maybe we can help each other? Maybe you can tell us more about... the Host?"

It darted back, up, to one side and then the other, pulled by that invisible string again. Then it hovered, as if waiting.

"Maybe.." Cotty began...

And then it was on her, instantly, it's grave-cold hands tearing at her dress, it's face gleeful with contempt and lust.

"No!" Art screamed, his hands passing through the thing as he tried to grapple with it. Useless, like trying to seize the winter wind.

Detestable-whore-trash-hurt-take

The images filled Cotty's mind, which translated them into words. She screamed, lashing out, clawing ineffectually at the spirit's eyes and face. How could it touch her when she couldn't touch it? It groped her breast, lips like ice water pressed against her own and a tongue like a gelid slug forced its way into her mouth. Distantly, she heard a gunshot, someone shouting. A hand wrapped itself around her wrist, pulled her free. The apparition darted back, glowering at her as Art dragged her away.

Somewhere in the distance there was an unearthly howl.

The spirit's head snapped in the direction of this sound, and then, just as quickly, it was gone, disappearing into the darkness.

"Oh God, oh God...!" Cotty gagged. Ripping her arm from Art's grasp she rolled over and brought up her last meal.

The others were at their side now, Jeremiah with both guns drawn, Johnny gripping a stick of dynamite he'd snatched from the crate.

"You okeh?" Johnny gasped.

"Okeh???" she shouted, trying in vain to spit the sensation of cold out of her mouth. *"I near been violated by the Ghost o' Christmas Past an' you ask if I'm okeh???"*

"Put that stick o' nitro down afore ya kill all of us!" Jeremiah snapped at Johnny.

"Sorry," Johnny said, immediately dropping the stick to the ground.

"No!" Jeremiah cried.

Cotty and Art gasped out loud, their hands instantly finding each other. Jeremiah, a lifelong atheist, was halfway through the Lord's Prayer when he realized that the stick had hit the ground without going off. It took all his willpower not to shoot Johnny right there, straight through the heart.

"Sorry," the easterner repeated sheepishly.

"They're not gonna help us," Cotty said. "They're *evil*. That's why this is happening to them. They... they *deserve* it."

"Can you walk?" Art asked her gently. She looked up at him like he was God's foremost anointed fool.

"Of course I can *walk*. Why wouldn't I be able to *walk*?"

Jeremiah sighed. Silently, he went ahead and finished that prayer.

卌 卌 卌 卌

BY THE TIME they reached the canyon the eastern horizon was already simmering with predawn light. The ghost hadn't returned, but more than once they heard it, or one of its ilk, shrieking in the night. Far more often they heard one of the great hounds' lonely howls. "Who's the *master* of them hounds, anyway?" Art asked at one point. Cotty assured him that he was better off not knowing. The plateau that the canyon cleaved in two appeared just barely climbable without any equipment, and Jeremiah cursed himself a fool for not thinking to bring at least a length of rope.

"So what's your plan?" Cotty asked.

"I'm thinking we ring th' top o' th' canyon on each side. That ought t' bring th' whole kit an' caboodle down inta th' pass and seal it up proper."

"But how do we get *this* up there?" Johnny asked. He almost toed the wagon for emphasis, just catching himself. Jeremiah turned slowly, and just as slowly drew on him.

"We don't need to get the crate up there, just

th' nitro, so I wuz thinkin' you'd load up yer pockets an' start climbin'."

Johnny blanched as he stared down the business end of Jeremiah's .44. Slowly he raised his eyes and met the gunslinger's gaze, at which point Jeremiah laughed long and loud.

"Damned fool," Jeremiah said, holstering his iron. "Yer freshly-soiled union suit is due payment fer dropping that stick o' nitro earlier." He turned to Art. "C'mon, Shakespeare, let's see an' if we c'n locate that door."

"I might've could've taken him," Johnny puffed up after they were out of earshot. "If it came to that. I'm a quick-draw, you know."

"Not something a gal likes to hear," Cotty said dismissively.

Carefully, guns drawn, the two men entered the canyon. Jeremiah held the lantern he carried in his off hand high, scanning the cliff walls carefully, searching... searching...

There.

"It wuz there," he said quietly, indicating a portion of the cliff face that looked no different from any other. Art shook his head.

"I don't..."

"I know." Jeremiah cocked his head, changed positions, tried to look at the space sideways. Nothing.

But Art was staring now, in wonderment.

"You just have to *insist*," he whispered. "Insist to yourself that it's there."

"Ya see it?"

"I do." He reached out with his left hand and made a strange motion, and suddenly they were awash in light-that-wasn't-light, a warm breeze enveloping them in the scent of a dewy summer morning. Art took a step forward.

"No," Jeremiah said, placing a hand on his shoulder. Art shook it off.

"I have to know," he said. "I have to *see*." He stepped through the portal.

And found himself in a gently rolling, tree-spotted plain suffused in eternal twilight, the barest glow of a rising – or setting – sun visible in all directions, just beneath every horizon, transforming everything into a silhouette of itself; a realm of perpetual shadows. This impressed itself on him in the merest of instants, and he stepped back without hesitation through the "door", terrified and longing for the world he knew.

Johnny and Cotty had appeared, and the latter threw herself into his arms.

"Oh thank God you're all right!" she shouted. She squeezed him so tight that it hurt. It was much lighter out now, and his eyes struggled to adjust.

Johnny and Jeremiah were gently stashing nitro sticks in any nook and cranny that would hold them. "Thought we lost ya," Jeremiah said without looking at him.

"Lost me?" Art asked, baffled.

"You were gone for an hour," Johnny said. "At

least."

"I almost come in after you," Cotty said into his chest. She turned her head to glare at Jeremiah. "Only *he* wouldn't let me."

"No need fer two t' die when only one needs ta."

"We done here?" Johnny asked, inspecting their work.

"I think so." Jeremiah looked out across the desert. "We'll take up position there," he said, indicating a small rise not far off. "When this Fired-Up Host marches back inta their hidey-hole we'll trigger one stick and hopefully the fallin' rocks will start a chain re-action an' trigger th' rest."

"But we've got no blasting caps. How are we gonna trigger the first one?"

Jeremiah held up his six gun and grinned.

ₕₕₕ ₕₕₕ ₕₕₕ ₕₕₕ |

THEY TOOK UP POSITION behind the rise. The edge of the sun was just visible over the horizon, and they doused the lanterns.

"What if they don't come back?" Johnny asked.

"They'll come back," Cotty said.

"Yes," Art agreed. He was still visibly shaken. "I saw their world. Our sunlight must seem so harsh to them. Like poison." He was crying. Cotty, who was lying next to him, gave his hand a squeeze.

"There," Jeremiah said.

Something was coming.

Riders, a score of them, shrouded in a cloud of trailing mist and attended by a pack of enormous hounds similar to the one they'd encountered in town. Half again the size of any living man, their mounts were of a commensurate size, great stallions and – yes – *stags*, eyes cataract-blank, steam wafting from their nostrils. Art gasped out loud, for he was certain that he recognized some of the horses as George's own, altered and gigantified in some unknowable manner. Stallion or stag, their hooves never quite touched the ground, as if they strode upon a pathway of perfectly transparent glass. The riders themselves were lightly armored, but their heads were bare, and while they looked to be men, of a sort, they had an electric, primitive quality that hinted of wild, unexplored places forever lost to time and the ken of Man. The procession proceeded at a leisurely, unhurried pace, and yet, somehow, appeared to simultaneously move slower than itself, as if it were two processions in one, out of sync with both the present moment and each other. There was a strange underlying sense that the riders' appearance, progress, very nature, was all a lie. Remembering the door, Jeremiah squinted, cocked his head, demanded that his brain perceive them for what they really were. It was like trying to see something, clearly, through a rippling pool of water, and yet he could almost...

"My God, they're beautiful..." Cotty said, breaking his concentration. She grabbed Art and began to work at his trousers. She was trembling with anticipation.

"What are you *doing?*" Art gaped.

"Please!" she begged. "I *ache* for it! For them! Have me or I'll go to them!"

She was near to shouting now, so Jeremiah grabbed her and clamped a hand over her mouth. She struggled mightily, squirming and thrashing like a woman possessed. When his hand slipped a little, she bit it.

"She's done lost her mind!" Jeremiah exclaimed.

"Just give her what she wants," Johnny deadpanned, his eyes never leaving the unearthly procession before them.

"Damn it!" Jeremiah hissed as one of Cotty's wildly kicking feet struck him in a particularly sensitive area. The girl was crying now, her eyes imploring him to release her, her arms reaching after the otherworldly riders. "What is *wrong* with ya?"

"I feel it too," Art whispered. "Don't you, just a little? If those riders, well..." He blushed. "If, well, they were *ladies*..."

"Hold her," Jeremiah told Art.

The riders had passed their hiding place and were entering the canyon now. Art wrapped his arms around Cotty from behind, pinning her arms to her side. He blushed again, embarrassed to find himself aroused by her struggles. Realizing this, she eagerly ground her body against his, and suddenly let out a long, low, guttural moan that seemed to go on forever.

The riders stopped.

"Hell buckets," Jeremiah swore.

Heads were turned in their direction now.

"I love you, Art, I love you," Cotty was babbling. *"Please don't let me go to them. It's all pain to them, pain forever. They don't know no different. I'm not weak; you'd go to them too if they was females of their kind, you'd go an'*

94

you'd be weaker'n me because men're so much weaker, all men want t' do is fornicate it's all men can do..."

One of the dread riders reoriented his mount so that it was facing in their general direction.

"Oh, Jesus..." said Johnny.

"What I wouldn't give fer a Gatlin' gun right now," Jeremiah said through clenched teeth.

Silence then. No one spoke, no one even breathed. Even the wind had apparently fled. Jeremiah peeped over the rise. He stared at the riders and they stared back. After what felt like an eternity he glanced at Cotty, absently wondering why she'd stopped fussing, only to find her and Art kissing. But hungrily, sloppily, like animals, her legs wrapped around his waist, his hands clenching fistfuls of her hair as if hanging on for dear life, her hands under his shirt, raking his back bloody. Johnny gaped at the pair, the terrible riders all but forgotten.

When Jeremiah returned his attention to the canyon, the riders were gone.

"Damnation! Come on!" Jeremiah shouted, leaping over the rise. Johnny followed a moment later, the two of them tearing across the cracked earth between their hiding place and the bisected plateau.

When they got there, the canyon was empty.

"Where are they?" Johnny asked, breathing heavily. He wasn't used to running medium distances. Or short ones, for that matter.

"They're gone back." Jeremiah said. "An' shut

th' door behind 'em."

Johnny approached the unremarkable patch of canyon wall where the door had been. Gently, he placed the palm of his hand on the cool stone.

"Like it was never here," he whispered.

"It still *is* here," Jeremiah said. "They jest ain't allowin' us t' see it." The sticks of dynamite they'd planted were still in place. "We'll bury it, like we planned. With any luck they won't dig themselves out 'til Judgement Day."

"Okeh," Johnny nodded. "Who gets..."

Jeremiah would never be able to accurately perceive, in his mind's eye, the *thing* that burst out of the concealed door then. Many times, often in nightmares, he tried, tried for his own sake to wrap his head around it by diluting it into a variation on some terrestrial fish, or insect, or plant, or even some nightmarish combination of all of these. But there was nothing, nothing in his experience (or, he suspected, in that of any sane man who had ever walked the earth) that could quantify what he saw that day. Even its *shape* eluded him. He knew only that when it retreated back into that portal, it took the top half of Johnny Love with it, and left the bottom half behind, geysering blood into the air for several seconds before it toppled to the ground.

Aghast, Jeremiah backpedaled. The wrong way as it turned out, deeper into the canyon. Someone was screaming; a harsh, shrill sound. He knew it was himself, but he couldn't accept this so he lay the blame on Cotty. His six gun was in his hand and he pointed it, firing wildly. Then, remembering the dynamite, he fired at one of the sticks, missing it, blasting a chip of stone out of the canyon wall. How many shots had he fired? He didn't know. Johnny's legs lay on the canyon floor, kicking and twitching as though alive. The door in the canyon wall was still open. *It* was coming, coming back.

He aimed at the door, pulled the trigger.

There was a dry click.

No... no...

No.

No, he had a second six gun. He drew it, reined in his panic.

Located one of the cached sticks of dynamite.

Fired.

Missed.

Concentrate, concentrate...

It was coming through the door, ebbing, crawling, flowing, all at once...

He ignored it, concentrated on the nitro.

He pulled the trigger.

The explosion brought down a cascade of rocks that struck other sticks, causing more explosions, more cascades, still more explosions, more cascades, explosions, cascades, forever.

Dust and rubble and a painful pressure in his ears: this was briefly his entire world, until there was nothing but a sense of overwhelming weight and a high-pitched ringing, and then darkness, and then, blessedly, nothing.

$$\text{IIII IIII IIII IIII II}$$

THE SUN was high in the sky when he opened his eyes. Was it later the same day, or after noon of the next? He didn't know, but it took him another day to dig himself out of the rubble and crawl up and over the mountain of loose rock that now sealed off the little canyon. His left wrist was broken, and he couldn't hear out of his right ear. But he was alive, and the mysterious door was now buried under several tons of stone. He'd chalk this one up as a win.

As soon as the lower edge of the sun kissed the western horizon, be began walking back to town.

He expected to find the others there, and maybe even the Army, alerted by folks passing through that something was amiss in Outskirts, Arizona. But no, the only living thing to be found in Outskirts was one of George's horses, returned after running off during the storm. In his subsequent travels he was always alert for news of one or more of them – Art, Cotty, George – but none was ever forthcoming. Many lifetimes later, while leafing through a disreputable story magazine at a newsstand in Boston, Massachusetts, he would stumble across a story entitled "The Terrible Tumbleweeds", credited to a Mr. Harry Frost. While coated with a necessary sheen of grounded plausibility, the events in this story would ring so familiar that he would write to the magazine, requesting the author's address. They never wrote back.

But there was nothing for it now. Taking care with his injured wrist, Jeremiah deftly mounted the returned horse. "I'm gonna call ya *Spec'utive Fiction*," he told the animal, before spurring her in the direction of Yuma.